The Open House

Will Eno

A SAMUEL FRENCH ACTING EDITION

FOUNDED 1830

SAMUELFRENCH.COM
SAMUELFRENCH-LONDON.CO.UK

FOR PRODUCTION ENQUIRIES

UNITED STATES AND CANADA
Info@SamuelFrench.com
1-866-598-8449

UNITED KINGDOM AND EUROPE
Plays@SamuelFrench-London.co.uk
020-7255-4302

Each title is subject to availability from Samuel French, depending upon
country of performance. Please be aware that *THE OPEN HOUSE* may
not be licensed by Samuel French in your territory. Professional and
amateur producers should contact the nearest Samuel French office or
licensing partner to verify availability.

MUSIC USE NOTE

Licensees are solely responsible for obtaining formal written permission from copyright owners to use copyrighted music in the performance of this play and are strongly cautioned to do so. If no such permission is obtained by the licensee, then the licensee must use only original music that the licensee owns and controls. Licensees are solely responsible and liable for all music clearances and shall indemnify the copyright owners of the play(s) and their licensing agent, Samuel French, against any costs, expenses, losses and liabilities arising from the use of music by licensees. Please contact the appropriate music licensing authority in your territory for the rights to any incidental music.

IMPORTANT BILLING AND CREDIT REQUIREMENTS

If you have obtained performance rights to this title, please refer to your licensing agreement for important billing and credit requirements.

THE OPEN HOUSE was first produced by the Signature Theatre at the Romulus Linney Courtyard Theatre in New York City on February 11, 2014. The performance was directed by Oliver Butler, with sets by Antje Ellermann, costumes by Bobby Frederick Tilley II, lighting by David Lander, sound by M.L. Dogg. The Production Stage Manager was Donald Fried. The cast was as follows:

DAUGHTER.	Hannah Bos
UNCLE	Michael Countryman
FATHER.	Peter Friedman
SON	Danny McCarthy
MOTHER.	Carolyn McCormick

CHARACTERS

*Each actor plays two roles, though only
the first character should be listed in the program.*

FATHER and **CHARLES** – late 50s-60s

MOTHER and **MELISSA** – late 50s-60s

DAUGHTER and **ANNA** – late 20s-30s

SON and **TOM** – late 20s-30s

UNCLE and **BRIAN** – 50s-60s

SETTING

A family room, somewhat drably and monochromatically decorated and wallpapered (beige?), not particularly beautifully lit. A couch, center, and an upholstered chair, stage left. Some small end tables. A door to the outside, upstage right. A bay window, with the curtains and shades drawn. A stairway, upstage. A closet door, stage left. A door, upstage, to another room. Perhaps there's an old dog bed downstage to the side somewhere. This is a normal family room, in a normal house.

PRODUCTION NOTES FROM THE PLAYWRIGHT

In the original Signature Theatre production of the play, director Oliver Butler and the cast created an opening moment in which, as the house lights were fading, Mother wheeled Father onto stage, accompanied by a very nice sound cue of classical music and New-England-ish sounds, such as lawnmowers and bicycle bells and birds. Once Father was in his spot, and Mother was seated in her chair, the lights faded down to black, and then, just three or four seconds later, the lights bumped up, as the music cue sharply ended, to reveal everyone, with Uncle (standing), and Daughter and Son (seated on the couch) being very still. There was a nice pause before Mother's first line. The three actors got onto stage in just slightly less time than one would think was physically possible. I found this to be a very strong, simple, and also startling beginning of the play. If directors want to do something different, I hope that they and their actors can find an opening moment that is simple and straightforward, but also slightly jarring, as this was.

In the first part of the play, where we meet the original family, there is probably not a lot of motion – the Father presides over the room from his wheelchair, the Mother (sincerely) offers food and drink, but never rises to get it, the Uncle remains standing, moving quietly and unnoticeably around the room, like a guest at a fancy party he wasn't directly invited to, and the Daughter and Son try to act as if they belong, but remain alert and wary. Probably, it is a "shoes off" sort of household. Despite the stillness, there is still a lot of tension, as each tries to manage the circumstance of "today," which is both new, because of Father's recent episode and because they are not often all together, and ancient, as they have all related to each other in a similar way for many years.

A thought on the Father character: it would probably be easy to make him into a cartoon, but it is best if he is played, instead, as a real person who just happens to be highly unkind and uncaring. He is someone who is probably in constant low-grade pain, and has needs just like the rest of the family, though he is unable to recognize and state those needs clearly. He inflicts his cruelty with minimal effort. If he can hurt someone with a word or two, sharply delivered, he will do it that way, rather than raising his voice and showing demonstrable anger.

A thought on the Mother character: she generally believes herself to be a caring and good mother, but perhaps because of her circumstances, she has developed some very deep defenses, so that, though her delivery may sound caring and concerned, she establishes very hard and strict limits on what can and cannot be said, on what feelings and emotional areas are allowed in the house.

Though there may be a formality and even a crispness to the way the family speaks to each other, they are also just human beings, trying to deal with life and each other. By that I mean to say that actors must find, as they always must find, a way to speak the lines so that they just sound like people.

When Anna, played by the actress who plays Daughter, enters, this is the beginning of a profound transformation, though it should begin slyly and quietly. That is, she should not charge in and immediately start transforming the room. In the Signature Theatre production, we used some magic battery-powered fake flowers that bloomed over the course of the last half-hour of the play. I'm sure many people did not notice this, but I mention it because I think attention to little details like this, things that slowly and almost unnoticeably accumulate, so that by the end of the play, the audience is looking at a different room filled with different people, can make for a very powerful experience.

I have heard interesting things from people about what *The Open House* represents. Some people have said it was the story of being born into one family, and perhaps through a husband or wife or through loving friends, finding yourself in another happier family. Some people have said it was about depression and how it can feel like the world is one seemingly unchanging beige room, without much air or movement in it, that slowly changes and becomes miraculously something colorful and hopeful. Some people have said it was a hard and true view of the very real Darwinian process that all of us participate in, in which we are here, and then suddenly, we are gone, replaced by other people. Somebody sent me a video about the Multiverse Theory and others mentioned Reincarnation. I think a simple but very detailed and specific production is best, in terms of evoking and allowing for these varied responses.

to the fleeting but perfect family of the Signature Theatre production

THE OPEN HOUSE

(Lights up on **MOTHER, FATHER, DAUGHTER, SON,** *and* **UNCLE.***)*

*(***FATHER** *is in a wheelchair and has a blanket over his legs.)*

(He is reading a newspaper.)

(See production notes, for details related to the play's opening moment.)

MOTHER. Well, I'll just say it again, it's wonderful having you all here.

(Pause. A dog barks, off-stage.)

FATHER. Would someone let the dog in.

SON. I'll get her.

*(***SON** *exits through the door, closes it. Calls out something that sounds like a dog's name.)*

(from off-stage, muffled:) Vrallen!

(He whistles and claps.)

DAUGHTER. Does anyone want anything? Coffee or anything?

MOTHER. I should be offering *you* a cup of coffee.

DAUGHTER. *(brief pause)* So, is there some?

SON. *(from off-stage, muffled:)* Hey girl!

DAUGHTER. Is there any already made?

MOTHER. Your father and I stopped drinking it. There might be some tea, though.

DAUGHTER. That's all right. Do you have any herbal tea?

MOTHER. I can take a look.

*(**SON** jiggles door handle, from outside, knocks quietly a couple times. This is a household where the door is always locked. **UNCLE** opens door for him. He re-enters.)*

FATHER. *(looking at **SON**)* Sorry – all I see is a human being.

SON. She's gone. The dog's gone.

DAUGHTER. She was just there.

FATHER. Did you close the door?

SON. Yeah.

MOTHER. Is she under the porch?

FATHER. I'm supposed to be resting.

SON. No, I looked under there.

FATHER. I'm not supposed to get upset.

DAUGHTER. *(to **FATHER**:)* We can find the dog without you getting upset.

FATHER. *(getting upset:)* And how is that?

MOTHER. Well, we're just going to have to –

FATHER. *(interrupting:)* Just going to have to, what? Oh, I'd love to hear how that ends.

MOTHER. We'll find the dog. It's not the end of the world.

FATHER. Who said anything about the... my God. Doesn't anyone in this family... And so now I guess she just upped and magically... I can't breathe. God... Can somebody please –

*(**DAUGHTER** moves to him.)*

DAUGHTER. Are you all right?

*(**FATHER** regains his composure, returns to his newspaper:)*

FATHER. I'm okay. If anyone cares.

DAUGHTER. I came right to your side.

MOTHER. I didn't think you wanted anyone to embarrass you.

DAUGHTER. I asked right away if you were all right.

FATHER. Yes, we all heard you say that. Let's move on. *(to* **SON***:)* Now, what were you going on about?

SON. *(normally)* I just said, "She's gone."

MOTHER. Okay but you don't have to get angry.

SON. Why do you think I'm – . I went out there and looked and then I came back in.

FATHER. I forgive you, son.

SON. For what?

FATHER. Let me get back to this, okay? *(disappears behind newspaper)*

MOTHER. She seemed fine the other day.

FATHER. *(from behind newspaper)* She's a very smart dog.

MOTHER. We could probably start without her. Listen to me: "start without her." Like she's a stenographer or something.

FATHER. Start what?

MOTHER. But she's family, you know? She should be here. *(to* **FATHER***:)* I didn't mean to say "start."

UNCLE. *(Brief general pause. His first line:)* She'll come back.

FATHER. Well, hello there. What's the matter – cat let go of your tongue? *(brief pause)* What's the matter – cat got your tongue?

UNCLE. I was, no, I was trying to say something positive.

FATHER. Just try to keep your tongue away from the cat, okay?

UNCLE. Okay. All you had to do was ask.

MOTHER. We don't have a cat. *(very brief pause)* Although, there was a time this whole place was a zoo. Remember? You all brought home every little wounded thing and asked if we could keep it. *(to* **DAUGHTER***:)* You were so cute with that rabbit that got hit by the car. You carried it around the house and said, "It's hurt, just like me." It was like an animal hospital around here.

DAUGHTER. I wasn't trying to be cute.

MOTHER. No, I know.

FATHER. A zoo or an animal hospital? Because you said both.

UNCLE. I remember thinking all those animals might contribute to a, or, just, I thought it would give the kids a good sense of animals.

FATHER. How many times do I have to ask you to never think about this family?

UNCLE. *(very brief pause)* This is actually the first I'm hearing of it.

FATHER. *(sounding sincere:)* Oh, sorry – I thought I'd asked you about that.

MOTHER. She turned up in a snowstorm. A little puppy on the doorstep in the snow.

DAUGHTER. *(to FATHER:)* Do you remember that?

FATHER. One of the happiest days of my life. *(to SON:)* What are you looking at?

UNCLE. Lot of good memories bundled up in that animal. She did get nervous, though. With the peeing and the shaking.

FATHER. That was probably because of the previous owners. Who knows what kind of a household she ran away from. *(to SON:)* What were you looking at?

MOTHER. That was the happiest day of your life?

(She takes out a pill from a pill bottle and puts it and a glass of water in front of FATHER.)

I'm going to miss that dog.

DAUGHTER. She hasn't been gone that long. Maybe she went for a walk.

FATHER. The dog can walk herself? What have I been doing all these years?

(He takes his pill and drinks some water.)

SON. What did you think you were doing?

FATHER. I don't know – stunting your growth?

MOTHER. Nobody stunted anybody's anything.

SON. *(brief pause)* I'm going to take another look.

(He exits.)

(as before:) Vrallen!

(He whistles and claps.)

DAUGHTER. It's good to be home. *(brief pause)* I don't think there's a rule that says we have to wait here in silence.

FATHER. *(Brief pause. Staring at her.)* No?

(Brief pause. **SON** *enters holding a chewy dog toy.)*

SON. Yeah, she's gone. There's just this thing she was chewing on and some fur stuck in the fence.

FATHER. Who are you, Sherlock Holmes?

SON. I'm just telling you what I saw.

FATHER. No, seriously – I don't know who you are. Is your name Sherlock?

SON. *(earnestly and with some concern:)* I'm your son.

FATHER. *(brief pause)* What do you want, a medal?

DAUGHTER. She loves all those chewy things.

MOTHER. I did not think I'd spend today thinking about *this*.

FATHER. Well, we've done everything we can. I mean, I haven't. I certainly haven't. *(to* **SON***:)* Forget what I said.

MOTHER. Maybe we should have a conversation about getting another dog. Oh, I'll miss her.

DAUGHTER. Shouldn't we just go look for her, first?

UNCLE. I'll go out in a bit. We'll find her. Ouch. Splinter.

(He's suddenly noticed a splinter in his hand, and begins trying to get it out.)

But, you know, old house, splintery banisters. No one to blame but myself.

FATHER. Exactly. *(brief pause)* What's today?

DAUGHTER. Tuesday. *(or whatever day it presently is.)*

FATHER. It feels like a Thursday *(or whatever is two days later)*.

DAUGHTER. It's Tuesday.

FATHER. I heard you. Why did I get out of bed?

MOTHER. Well, it's our anniversary.

FATHER. Other than that.

DAUGHTER. Isn't that enough of a reason? And we came home to see you.

SON. Happy anniversary.

DAUGHTER. *(handing* **MOTHER** *a wrapped gift)* Yeah, happy anniversary, Mom and Dad.

MOTHER. Oh, you shouldn't have done that. Thank you, okay? I mean it. It's very thoughtful. Well, this is just a delight.

(She sets the gift down, unopened.)

(to **FATHER***:)* See? You got out of bed for all this celebration.

FATHER. How long have we been married? Wait, don't tell me. *(He goes back to reading his newspaper.)*

MOTHER. *(brief pause)* Are you going to try?

FATHER. Try what?

MOTHER. Are you going to try guessing how long?

FATHER. I'm sure it's written down somewhere.

UNCLE. *(trying to remove the splinter)* Time is crazy. One minute, you're standing on the deck of an ocean liner with your heart beating out of your chest and all the smoke and cathedrals of Europe at your back... *(distracted by the splinter)* I hope this isn't infected... it looks like it's really been in there for a while. *(removes splinter)* There we go. I think I got it.

MOTHER. Oh, good. Do you want some of that first-aid spray?

UNCLE. No, I'll just make sure to wash up. *(brief pause)* Auughh. This is so frustrating – now there's this song I can't get out of my head.

FATHER. *(very brief pause)* I don't hear anything.

UNCLE. I feel like I'm possessed. It just keeps going around and around and, actually, wow – it's gone.

FATHER. Do you really have to say things? Would the world stop?

UNCLE. Probably not. Although, not to be funny, but, who's to say that the world –

FATHER. *(interrupting:)* Somebody else! Somebody else!

DAUGHTER. But, so, yeah, congratulations.

MOTHER. Well, thank you, okay? I remember one year, on our Anniversary, we went – I was so surprised— but, your father took me out to –

FATHER. *(interrupting:)* I had French Onion soup.

MOTHER. You remember?

FATHER. Now you're questioning me?

MOTHER. I'm asking you a question.

FATHER. *(to no one in particular:)* Do you see what I have to put up with?

UNCLE. Who are you talking to?

FATHER. Not you.

SON. That's the same restaurant that...*(quietly but sharply, in pain, as he tries to straighten out his body on the couch:)* Jesus. Owww.

FATHER. It'll pass, son. *(very brief pause)* Whatever it is.

SON. Wow. Sorry. God. I had a leg cramp.

FATHER. We don't need to know the details.

MOTHER. Are you all right? You know, I just remembered, Lucy Paquette had terrible leg cramps.

DAUGHTER. Who's Lucy Paquette?

FATHER. Your mother learns people's names and then when one of you kids gets hurt or has some feelings, she'll talk about that person for a while.

MOTHER. Now that's just ridiculous.

FATHER. You know what, don't listen to me. *(sort of an imitation of Darth Vader:)* "I'm your father."

MOTHER. And who are you now? Is that one of your impressions? *(brief pause)* Sometimes, they kept her up all night. Lucy. Doctors said it was a potassium deficiency.

FATHER. *(said as if he means "I rest my case":)* Cogito ergo sum.

UNCLE. Don't you mean *Quod Erat Demonstrandum*?

FATHER. You're still here?

DAUGHTER. *(to* **UNCLE***:)* I always thought it was great you learned Latin.

UNCLE. They said I was a fool to study Latin, but, where are they now?

FATHER. Probably at work.

UNCLE. We had to pick a new language or a hobby. It was a big part of my recovery.

FATHER. Yes, it was. And you've done very well with that.

UNCLE. *(Brief pause. Waiting for sarcasm.)* Thank you. I thought you were going to make fun of me.

FATHER. Yeah, I don't know what happened there. But anyway, yeah, you did good.

MOTHER. *(to* **UNCLE***:)* Yes, huzzah, for how you faced that whole part of your life, okay? Huzzah. Anyway, that year on our anniversary, we went out for the most wonderful lunch. What was the name of that place? It was right down the street from that couple.

FATHER. The Rusty Scupper.

MOTHER. The Rusty Scupper. And what was their name? It sounded Greek but it wasn't.

FATHER. Temos.

MOTHER. Temos. Holly and Paul Temos. There was a little lake out in front of the restaurant and I remember the light, we went at the perfect time of day, and it was just so pretty, with the light just kind of –

FATHER. *(interrupting:)* Opalescent.

MOTHER. What? Opalescent? I guess it was that. That's my spokesman, over there. Holly and Paul took care of the dog, when your father was in the hospital, last year. They didn't call me back, this time. They loved having her, though.

DAUGHTER. Why didn't they call back?

MOTHER. Do you know what, I'm not sure. I don't think it's a very happy home, so they're probably busy with that. *(to* **FATHER***:)* Did you see, I set out a coat and tie for you.

FATHER. Don't call me "dear."

DAUGHTER. She didn't.

FATHER. I know, I'm just saying, don't. And I can dress myself.

MOTHER. Well, you do have some trouble. It's nothing to be embarrassed about, we all need a little help.

FATHER. You always thought you were very helpful.

MOTHER. Is that – I don't know what you're saying.

FATHER. Nothing. *(He ends the following so it sounds like a diminishing echo.)* I am saying nothing – nothing, nothing, nothing.

MOTHER. So now you're, what, you're pretending you're a canyon? I don't know how he wants me to react. *(with some positivity:)* But, I guess it keeps things interesting. *(A general pause. No one responds.* **SON** *coughs or clears his throat, quietly.)*

DAUGHTER. *(to* **MOTHER***:)* What were you going to say about the lunch place?

MOTHER. Oh, I don't know. *(very brief pause)* You know, the second I woke up, I felt, ah, this is a Tuesday *(or whatever day it is)*. But it also felt special. And I wanted it to be special. I was having an egg in the kitchen and the birds were chirping and I was getting ready to read my book. Then your father made some comment about how ugly the sunrise was and how he hated the smell of paper. And all the muscles in my back just knotted right up.

DAUGHTER. You should get a massage.

FATHER. Maybe I should, yeah.

DAUGHTER. I meant Mom.

FATHER. It's not important who you meant.

MOTHER. And this is my life. I sat there and thought, "Is this really my life?" Do you know I was a tomboy, when I was a girl?

FATHER. As you know, I'm not a talkative man, but, since we're all here… The day I met your mother, it was a day very like today, a normal day –

DAUGHTER. *(interrupting:)* No, Dad, come on.

FATHER. A normal day with nothing especially promising in sight. Other than a girl in the distance in a hat and dress. She was beautiful and I wanted to say something. Hello, I said. It just came to me, right off the top of my head. Hello, she said. We walked into the Boston Common. We watched the swan boats. I held her hand in the sun. I was so happy. The day, like every other, no matter whether it's unlike any other, ended. We bid adieu. On the way home, I met your mother here. We talked a little, probably went out to dinner a few times. Then her mother died of pneumonia and we got married. Hence, you two. And my brother became an uncle. His only accomplishment— correct me if I'm wrong – to date. And there we are, in a nutshell. Your origin story.

UNCLE. I've had other accomplishments.

*(**FATHER** chuckles to himself.)*

DAUGHTER. *(to **MOTHER**)* Doesn't it bother you when he talks like that?

MOTHER. Well, to be honest, it does. He always tells it differently and I always hope it's going to be me in the first part. *(to **FATHER**:)* But, I've grown accustomed to your voice. "Accustomed" isn't the right word.

FATHER. It's a true story – what can I do?

DAUGHTER. Not tell it?

FATHER. Actually, okay, you've got a point.

DAUGHTER. And it's not a true story, anyway.

FATHER. It captures the general feeling.

SON. Since we're talking about this, there's a lot of different ways we could be toward each other.

(**FATHER** *stares at* **SON** *for a moment, then yawns.*)

FATHER. *(quietly:)* Whoo. Tired.

MOTHER. *(Brief pause. To* **DAUGHTER***:)* Did you come straight from the airport? Have you eaten?

DAUGHTER. I drove here. It's a half-hour away. I don't live in Morganville, anymore.

MOTHER. No, of course, I know that. But have you eaten?

DAUGHTER. I'm fine.

FATHER. *(gently, as if it's fatherly advice:)* Maybe some young man makes you feel like you are, briefly, but, late at night, by yourself, you know it's not the case. You know you're not fine.

DAUGHTER. There's no reason for you to say things like that.

FATHER. No, and yet, here we are.

DAUGHTER. Well, it really hurts.

FATHER. So don't do it.

DAUGHTER. Don't do what?

FATHER. I'm sure they're just jealous.

DAUGHTER. Who?

FATHER. *(something in the newspaper has caught his eye)* Huh. *(He reads.)* "Councilwoman Wanda Perkova to be replaced."

SON. Who's Wanda Perkova?

FATHER. Well, I guess it doesn't matter anymore, does it.

UNCLE. *(brief pause)* Do you know that thing about, "A guy's got to do what a guy's got to do"? I just read this pretty long article about how scientists have discovered that, in fact, no, actually, he doesn't.

FATHER. *(said with enthusiasm, as if he's saying "Interesting.")* Uninteresting.

UNCLE. We think we have to be some certain way, you know?

FATHER. *(amiably agreeing:)* Why can't we just be happy being who we are?

UNCLE. Well, yeah – right.

FATHER. *(stares at* **UNCLE***)* It's so hard to find your way. Speaking of all this, you ever seen this one? It's kind of a fun little parlor trick. *(He goes back to his newspaper. Brief pause. Quietly:)* Ta-da!

DAUGHTER. *(long pause)* Why are we like this?

FATHER. "We"? And what makes you think we're like something? Like what?

DAUGHTER. Like this.

(Pause. Silence and stillness, from everyone, perhaps an air of tension and anxiety.)

MOTHER. It's so quiet.

DAUGHTER. What were we like as kids?

MOTHER. You were kids. I don't know. You were great. It's so nice you're all here.

FATHER. You've said that three times, now. It's obviously not that nice, because if it were, then you'd probably just be enjoying the fact, instead of anxiously asserting that it's true.

MOTHER. I'm not asserting anything. And, I don't "do" anxiety, okay? I'm just saying I cherish you all. I cherish you right down to your bones.

FATHER. That's kind of a cold word, isn't it? "Cherish"?

MOTHER. Well, but I mean it, okay?

DAUGHTER. It's good to be home.

FATHER. Yeah, keep saying that. *(very brief pause)* Kind of a greeting card word, "cherish," if you ask me.

SON. *(quietly:)* Nobody did.

MOTHER. I think it's a fine word. "Cherish."

FATHER. *(to* **SON***:)* What did you just say? Excuse me? *(very brief pause)* I know why you're all here. Vultures.

DAUGHTER. How are we vultures?

FATHER. You're here to be nice to me.

DAUGHTER. And?

SON. Yeah, how does that make us vultures?

FATHER. I've raised a bunch of poor people.

DAUGHTER. What?

FATHER. You don't have any money. You're poor. *(brief pause)* You are here to pretend to care, to appear to be kind, so that I don't write you out of the will.

MOTHER. That's ridiculous. As if we've got some huge secret estate. Everyone was worried about you, okay?

DAUGHTER. I don't know why you'd even think that.

FATHER. Assuming I ever wrote you *into* the will.

MOTHER. *(to DAUGHTER and SON:)* Don't worry. You're both very well taken care of.

FATHER. Actually, I changed that.

MOTHER. He's just trying to be threatening.

DAUGHTER. Why would you want to be threatening?

FATHER. *(gently, and with care)* It's not a threat, sweetie. Trust me. Please, I just need you to trust me on this.

DAUGHTER. That you've taken us out of your will?

FATHER. Exactly. Yes. *(to SON:)* It *is* good to talk about these things, isn't it?

UNCLE. *(points to a chair)* Who gets this?

MOTHER. He has a hard time saying how much he loves you.

FATHER. No, I don't.

DAUGHTER. That isn't what we came home for.

FATHER. No?

DAUGHTER. *(Brief pause. To MOTHER:)* Mom, the yard looks nice.

MOTHER. I try to get out there when I can. I think you all brought the good weather with you.

DAUGHTER. Yeah, we should open the curtains.

FATHER. Keep those closed.

MOTHER. It might be nice to get some sun in here.

FATHER. *(flare-up of anger)* It's not the most complicated idea: bright sun ruins furniture.

MOTHER. I don't think one afternoon of sun would hurt anything.

FATHER. Why don't we just throw it all in a bonfire in the backyard?

MOTHER. Nobody wants to light anything on fire.

FATHER. No?

DAUGHTER. Could we just not fight.

MOTHER. Nobody's fighting.

SON. I wish we did fight.

FATHER. No you do not.

DAUGHTER. Someday, we're not going to be like this anymore.

SON. *(brief pause)* So, can I say something here?

MOTHER. Of course. You can say anything you like. You can talk about the King of Norway, if you want. You know that. Although I hope it's not something about how I'm a terrible mother or how we need to fight. I know you'd never say anything like that.

DAUGHTER. *(to* **SON***:)* Remember, today was just supposed to be about relaxing and being together.

FATHER. Let him talk. What shall my only son pronounce?

MOTHER. What do you mean, your only son? What about Richard?

FATHER. *(quiet but real disdain, as if someone just suggested a food he finds disgusting:)* Bleaghhk.

UNCLE. How is Richard?

DAUGHTER. I haven't talked to him for like a year.

MOTHER. I think he's very busy. *(to* **SON***:)* You should call him sometime, you know? That's just being a good brother.

DAUGHTER. I left him a message for his birthday.

FATHER. Oh, I bet he enjoyed that. *(to* **SON***:)* Weren't you going to say something?

SON. I was just wondering, like…

FATHER. *(brief pause)* "Like." The curse of your generation. I'm, like, sitting here. That wall is, like, beige. Eventually, all distinctions will disappear for you. And you will be, like, gone. *(He starts to chew a fingernail.)* Ouch. Cuticle. Maybe I should use one of those hand creams. *(to SON:)* You know, to moisturize the skin. To prevent dryness. In the hands. *(very brief pause)* Why do I bother opening up my heart to you.

MOTHER. I have hand cream upstairs. Now, is anyone hungry? *(to SON:)* Are you okay? Do you want a nice soup or something?

SON. I'm all right.

FATHER. *(returning to newspaper)* It's supposed to rain.

MOTHER. *(to SON:)* Oh, now don't slump. Sit up nice and straight, son. Let everyone see you.

FATHER. Yeah, let me take a look at my boy. *(He stares for a moment, returns to his newspaper.)* They say we need it, though – rain.

MOTHER. *(brief pause)* Was there any mail out there? I can't remember if I looked, yesterday.

FATHER. What if we got something urgent?

(DAUGHTER *gets up to check.)*

MOTHER. I forgot. Are you expecting something?

FATHER. That's why you look. To see if something is there.

DAUGHTER. *(having leaned out the door to look)* Nope, no mail.

FATHER. See? Now we know.

MOTHER. Just as well. All the terrible news. Who needs it. It's funny. I mean, yes, people can be barbaric, absolutely barbaric.

DAUGHTER. *(very brief pause)* But?

MOTHER. Sorry, hon?

DAUGHTER. People are barbaric, *but?* I thought you were going to say something more.

MOTHER. Well, I never know what you want me to say. And with your father always glaring at me.

FATHER. I stopped glaring at you years ago. *(brief pause)* I'm a real one-note-Johnny, aren't I? Always so cutting and sarcastic.

MOTHER. Is that an apology?

FATHER. I love how your mind works.

MOTHER. *(picking up her book)* Oww. My wrist.

DAUGHTER. You should get that looked at.

MOTHER. Well, I know I should, but, with your father and everything. *(She tries moving her wrist.)* Oww. This just does not go away. Oh, I don't want to read, anyway. That book is just all words. No, but it's interesting. It follows the whole lineage of Scandinavian Royalty. Denmark, Norway, all around there. There was a Viking king named Gorm the Old. *(to* **SON***:)* Would you like it if we had named you "Gorm the Old"? Anyway, there's this whole part about his burial chamber. I guess it was a burial mound, really, which, from tree-dating and carbon, you know, the rings on the trees, they put the date at 958 AD. They found a skeleton in it, a man they think was about five foot seven, but they don't think it was Gorm. All the gold and jewelry was gone, too. Isn't that funny – graverobbers, way back then, people doing things wrong, thousands of years ago. Imagine robbing a grave. Is nothing sacred? His son was Harold. There were a lot of Karls and Margrets too.

DAUGHTER. *(brief pause)* What made you start reading that?

MOTHER. Someone left it here. *(referring to her wrist, as she flexes it:)* This is all right. It's just kind of "there," you know?

(Very distant sound of an ambulance siren. No one stops to listen or pays it any attention.)

SON. There's that sports medicine clinic right near the church.

DAUGHTER. Dr. Eckstein. He's great. Remember I went to him when I was training for the marathon?

MOTHER. No, it's all right. It doesn't really bother me.

FATHER. *(brief pause)* The good thing about things like this –

UNCLE. *(interrupting:)* Things like what?

FATHER. Don't interrupt me.

UNCLE. I was just trying to define some terms.

FATHER. Yeah, well, don't. Not in my house.

MOTHER. It's funny the dog picked today to run away.

DAUGHTER. She'll come back.

UNCLE. I'm sure she will.

FATHER. Now I forgot what I was going to say. Wait. *(He listens intently.)* I just heard her collar jingle. Somebody go look.

*(**UNCLE** goes to the door, looks, returns.)*

UNCLE. *(in an Irish accent:)* Must've been only the wind.

MOTHER. *(amused)* What is that?

UNCLE. It's probably from a movie or something.

FATHER. So I was wrong, it wasn't the dog's collar. I can admit when I've made a mistake. *(refers to **MOTHER**:)* Exhibit A. *(refers to **SON** and **DAUGHTER**:)* Exhibits B and C. Hi, kids.

UNCLE. She probably just needed a little air. Dogs need air, right? And she always got shy when everyone was around.

MOTHER. Oh, she would've spent her whole life under that porch, if she could.

DAUGHTER. We all would have.

MOTHER. Is that a comment? You know, your father loved you all when you were little. It was only when you started to talk.

DAUGHTER. Isn't that an important time?

MOTHER. It was just when he didn't know what you'd say – that's when he didn't know what to do.

SON. *(to* **MOTHER***:)* What did you think, when we started talking?

MOTHER. Oh, it didn't really bother me. I mean, no – you kids were great. You know, with your father, I don't even hear him, sometimes. *(very brief pause)* I like this little old life of mine. I'm just very happy to be here with you all on this funny old planet.

SON. Yeah, me too. *(brief pause)* Actually, I just got a little hungry. Maybe some soup or something would be good.

MOTHER. Can you believe our little recipe club has been meeting for 22 years? I think that's, in this day and age, I think that's pretty impressive.

FATHER. *(to* **UNCLE***:)* I guess I can't really call *you* a mistake. Although I did agree to let you live here when your wife left.

UNCLE. She was killed in a tornado.

FATHER. Oh, right. That does sound familiar.

UNCLE. That's because it's what happened. I miss Melanie almost every day.

FATHER. *(an entirely sympathetic sound, as if* **UNCLE** *has said something cute:)* Aww. *(very brief pause)* Now, if you all wouldn't mind, just let me sit here for a minute. I need to rest my eyes. *(He closes his eyes.)*

UNCLE. *(Brief pause. Quietly:)* Do you guys remember Melanie?

MOTHER. *(quietly:)* Of course.

DAUGHTER. *(quietly:)* She helped me make a map of the neighborhood for school. It was so big I could barely carry it, even rolled up. Remember when I was always making maps? She wore high heels.

UNCLE. *(quietly:)* She did. She liked clothes. She said I had the right body for an Italian suit. She used to say such nice things to me. Even first thing, waking up. That felt good.

MOTHER. *(quietly:)* She was, just, she was a real ray of sunshine.

(DAUGHTER moves toward FATHER, to pull the blanket up around him.)

FATHER. Get away from me! Oh, it's just you. *(quietly and plainly:)* Try to keep this area clear.

DAUGHTER. I was just going to pull the blanket up.

MOTHER. He has dreams he's being murdered.

DAUGHTER. You do?

FATHER. I guess you're not going to let me sleep. *(Very brief pause. To MOTHER:)* You know, we should go out for a nice dinner. Just the two of us. Or, just me.

DAUGHTER. Do you want me to call somewhere and make a reservation?

FATHER. I'm not hungry.

SON. I have nightmares too.

FATHER. *(without any of his customary edge:)* Really?

SON. Yeah.

MOTHER. Well, "good life – bad dreams," isn't that what they say?

SON. I've never heard that.

DAUGHTER. Yeah, me neither. But it makes sense. You work through stuff in your sleep.

MOTHER. You kids were such funny sleepers. You both had a blanket you loved. *(to FATHER:)* Remember those blankets?

FATHER. *(again, without any edge:)* Remember what you did? *(to SON and DAUGHTER:)* She sewed them together.

MOTHER. I did, I knitted them together, because we could never keep track of you two and we thought it'd be easier. So you took your naps together, both of you holding onto your own half. I think Richard wished I knitted him one.

DAUGHTER. I remember that.

FATHER. Really? You were so small.

SON. Yeah, I think I remember it too.

FATHER. You both really loved that thing.

DAUGHTER. It was yellow and blue.

MOTHER. That's exactly right. It was gold and blue. You still both got very fussy, at bedtime. All you kids.

SON. *(to* **FATHER***:)* You used to smoke a pipe.

FATHER. Did I? *(very brief pause)* Work through this in your sleep. *(He makes his hand into a gun, points it at* **SON***.)* Bang.

SON. What does that mean?

FATHER. It's a very simple gesture, son.

DAUGHTER. *(brief pause)* Remember how little the dog was? I can still see her shivering on the stoop in the snow.

FATHER. Can you.

DAUGHTER. Yes.

FATHER. Are you trying to make it seem like things are okay?

DAUGHTER. Yes.

FATHER. Part of me admires you for that. The rest of me is just afraid of having another stroke.

UNCLE. She was so tiny when she was a pup.

MOTHER. We put that little red ribbon around her neck.

FATHER. I'm afraid. *(brief pause)* Did anyone hear me say that? I wish one of you could show a little sympathy.

MOTHER. Well, you make it very difficult.

FATHER. But not impossible. Not impossible.

SON. I know you're not feeling well.

FATHER. No, I'm not.

DAUGHTER. We all just came here to try to help, to try to make you feel better.

FATHER. Are you done?

DAUGHTER. Yes. *(very brief pause)* I don't know what you want from us.

FATHER. It's a real conundrum, isn't it. If only we could figure it out.

MOTHER. *(to* **SON** *and* **DAUGHTER***:)* He probably does need to eat.

FATHER. Yeah, maybe that's one of my needs: food. Can someone go look in a dictionary and see if humans eat food?

MOTHER. I'll make something in a minute. *(to* **FATHER***:)* Have you done your exercises?

FATHER. Yes.

SON. Grinding your teeth doesn't count.

(The others are quietly amused.)

MOTHER. *(to* **FATHER***:)* Have you, really?

FATHER. *(to* **SON***:)* Are you using humor to deal with the situation? Because, don't.

SON. Okay.

FATHER. And there's no situation, anyway. I don't know who you all think you are. I paid for all of this.

UNCLE. What are you gesturing to?

SON. I know. We know that.

DAUGHTER. We appreciate everything you've done.

FATHER. I'm sorry, everyone. Things are a little stressful – because I actually haven't done my exercises, because she didn't remind me.

DAUGHTER. So you can do them now. It's fine. Or whenever.

FATHER. *(to* **MOTHER***:)* You didn't remind me.

MOTHER. Well, I'm reminding you now.

FATHER. *(hatefully, but with no effort:)* I don't care. *(Brief pause. Musingly:)* You know, I bet if I had a little more charisma, this stuff would really fly. All this cruelty and negativity. What does everyone think about that? *(brief pause)* It's such a fine line, you know?

SON. *(brief pause)* Dinner was good, last night.

DAUGHTER. I'm sorry I missed it.

MOTHER. It came out well, didn't it.

SON. Yeah, it was great. Effi is a really good cook. I can't wait for you to meet her.

MOTHER. Well, thank you. Okay? I mean it.

SON. She and I cook together sometimes. We have a lot of fun.

MOTHER. Well, that's just a, that sounds like a real delight.

SON. I feel really calm with her.

FATHER. Your mother doesn't care, son.

MOTHER. I care.

FATHER. Then say something caring.

MOTHER. I can't just... I'm not a trained seal.

FATHER. Your mother is not a trained seal, son. And that's why she was unable to say, "I'm happy for you." Or, "You deserve love," or a single caring word. Like, as we all know, a trained seal would've done. Tell me about her. Tell your old pa about your new gal.

SON. Okay. So, she's in Med School, but she's thinking about getting into Public Policy.

FATHER. Good for her. Smart. What's she look like? I bet she's a real beauty.

MOTHER. *(to SON:)* I didn't want to embarrass you with a lot of questions.

SON. I swear, she's the most beautiful person. Just, the way she does everything, the way she walks through a grocery store or looks at the sky. It's like I sometimes can see the little girl in her and also the old lady, and then she looks at me and smiles, and, it's her, right there, just totally her.

FATHER. *(stares at him for a moment)* Did I take my medicine? I did, just remembered. *(going back to newspaper)* Answered my own question.

DAUGHTER. *(to SON:)* She sounds really nice.

SON. She is.

FATHER. *(behind newspaper.)* That's a good price for a car battery.

DAUGHTER. Would it... do you think you could read that later? We came all this way.

FATHER. I thought it was just a half-hour drive. But I should be giving you my full attention, shouldn't I.

MOTHER. From the outside, we probably wouldn't look perfect. But I think we're kind of figuring it out, you know? When I was a little girl, after dinner, my father would always gather us around –

FATHER. *(interrupting:)* You all think you're going to change things. You show up year after year, or for my strokes and heart attacks, always the same, always thinking I'm going to change. Do you see the irony? You never change. None of you ever changes. You think I owe you something. Life isn't enough. The gift of life isn't enough. Plus, you got clothes and food.

MOTHER. And he never hit you. He never hit any of you.

FATHER. Please, darling, now you're just making me blush.

DAUGHTER. I just would like it if we could, like, or, I sometimes wish I could ask you about things.

FATHER. Well, I can understand that.

SON. You do?

FATHER. I said I *can*. But, yes. So, go ahead.

DAUGHTER. What?

FATHER. Ask.

DAUGHTER. I don't have any big, I mean, I wasn't thinking we could just change overnight.

FATHER. Yeah, you were.

DAUGHTER. Can someone help me here.

MOTHER. I think you're doing great. And, I agree, we *can't* change overnight. But I think this is a good start. Let's call today a very good start.

FATHER. *(brief pause)* What are we doing about lunch?

MOTHER. I could make my three-bean salad.

FATHER. I have a fun idea – how about something better-tasting than that? *(to* **SON***:)* You have bones because I bought you baby formula. I even asked, at the store, "Does this have calcium in it?" Your mother felt breast-feeding would give you the wrong idea.

MOTHER. That's not what it was. At that time, they didn't recommend it.

SON. Who's "they?"

FATHER. That's my favorite thing you've said. Thatta boy, bare those teeth. *(Looks at* SON. *Very brief pause.)* You've got something on your... *(points to his own chin)*

*(*SON *wipes his mouth.)*

SON. Did I get it?

FATHER. *(having lost interest and returned to his newspaper)* I don't know.

MOTHER. It was not the tradition, at the time.

FATHER. The tradition of breast-feeding is millions of years old. A physiological and emotional bond, ancient and natural, almost as old as time itself, deeply entwined in our most basic sense of being human. And then a couple magazine articles came out, and your mother's mind was completely changed.

MOTHER. You said it was disgusting.

FATHER. You believed me.

MOTHER. You said we'd look like barn animals.

FATHER. Did I? Where do I come up with this stuff?

DAUGHTER. I can go over to the deli and get some sandwiches.

MOTHER. You don't have to do that – you just got here. Are you sure you want to go right back out?

DAUGHTER. Yeah, it'll just be quick.

FATHER. *(to* DAUGHTER:*)* Need a little reprieve? Going out to steel your nerves?

UNCLE. Some sandwiches sounds good.

MOTHER. Can I give you some money?

DAUGHTER. I think I'm all right.

(As she's putting on her jacket and shoes, she looks in her small purse and accidentally drops it. FATHER *laughs a small laugh.)*

What?

FATHER. Nothing. Right from the start, even when you were just learning to walk, you were always so clumsy.

DAUGHTER. I know. *(brief pause)* So, I wasn't going to say anything.

FATHER. And that would have been the right decision. *But?*

DAUGHTER. Dad… So, I just went to the doctor's. They found a bump on my spine. Near my spine. I was having a mammogram, and, that went okay, but then I had to go back. I'm supposed to hear next week.

(Brief pause. She's scared in a very deep and plain way and wants to lean on something.)

I wish there was a handrail here.

FATHER. It doesn't sound that serious.

MOTHER. It's good to have that all looked at.

DAUGHTER. It's not "that all." It's one particular thing. And it could be really serious.

MOTHER. Well, I'm "holding you," okay?

DAUGHTER. Okay. What does that mean?

FATHER. It's from the Quaker church, and it means: I'll hold you in my thoughts, in my heart, I'll be holding your hand throughout this. But since your mother's not a Quaker, it's just a way of saying "I'm holding you" without actually having to hold the person. *(looks at paper)* Is that *really* a good price for a car battery? You can't be too careful. Right, sweetie? I guess you've learned that.

DAUGHTER. How? Yes, I have. What?

MOTHER. It *is* from the Quaker church. And, I think it is a, well, I think it's a lovely idea. And I'm sorry if that's what I said and if it wasn't the right thing. But I mean it, okay?

DAUGHTER. Okay.

MOTHER. They do something they call "listening for the quiet voice of God." I've gone to several services with Monica and, what was her husband's name? It's a wonderful community.

FATHER. Joe. Joseph.

MOTHER. Joseph, exactly. He has that lawnmower-repair place. He and Monica were thinking of starting up a little gift store. But now they want to wait. But they still go around to different gift stores and souvenir shops and look for interesting ideas.

FATHER. *(to others:)* Did you get all that? You might want to write it down. Someone you don't know may or may not start up a gift store in a few years.

DAUGHTER. *(Brief pause. To* **FATHER***:)* Doesn't anyone else get to be scared?

FATHER. What?

DAUGHTER. Doesn't anyone else get to be scared and get to say stupid scared things?

FATHER. *(Brief pause. Gently:)* Of course, sweetheart. Clearly.

UNCLE. *(to* **DAUGHTER***:)* Just remember that thing: seven times down, eight times up.

DAUGHTER. Thanks.

SON. Do you want me to come with you? To the store?

DAUGHTER. Why is everything always a question? Why doesn't anyone ever just help?

SON. Those are questions right there.

DAUGHTER. *(wounded:)* Touché.

FATHER. I'm not supposed to eat red meat.

MOTHER. Maybe you can get him tuna fish or something like that?

DAUGHTER. Okay.

MOTHER. I'm sure whatever you get'll be fine. But no red meat for him. And don't get those wrapped things.

DAUGHTER. Do you want to just tell me and I can write it down?

MOTHER. Whatever you get'll be fine. *(Very brief pause. Compassionately:)* Oh, sweetie.

DAUGHTER. I'm scared.

MOTHER. Well, it's good you're getting it all checked out.

DAUGHTER. Yeah. *(to* SON*:)* Did you want to go?

SON. That's all right. I'll stay with these guys.

(Brief pause. UNCLE *moves toward* DAUGHTER*.)*

UNCLE. *(gently and compassionately:)* Do you need me to move my car?

DAUGHTER. No, I parked on the street. Okay. Is there anything else? *(brief pause)* Could someone please say something?

MOTHER. We'll be here when you get back.

(DAUGHTER *hesitates for a moment, then exits. Pause. The sound of her car starting, after several tries.)*

I wonder if she has what I have?

FATHER. How would I know?

SON. What do you have?

MOTHER. It's something women in my family are at a fairly high risk for.

FATHER. I should've asked for iced tea.

MOTHER. I can call. Why don't I call her?

SON. *(to* FATHER*:)* You should talk to Effi about diet. She's really studied that stuff.

MOTHER. Well, I think we've got it all figured out.

SON. What were you saying before?

MOTHER. Your father doesn't like when I talk about it.

FATHER. You can talk about whatever you want. *(brief pause)* I just wouldn't mind some clam chowder once in a while.

MOTHER. *(to* SON*:)* But thank you, though, okay?

UNCLE. A bump on the spine. "Near the spine" – that seems even worse.

MOTHER. Oh, I know. I'm glad they're not worried about it.

UNCLE. Who said they weren't worried about it?

MOTHER. They said they just wanted to check it all out. *(to* FATHER*:)* I think you can have a little clam chowder.

FATHER. I'll listen to what the doctor said.

MOTHER. Well then you should do your exercises.

FATHER. Can someone push me, please?

MOTHER. He likes doing them back there.

SON. We could set up the laundry room so you could do them in there.

(He wheels him upstage, so that he faces away from the audience.)

FATHER. That would not be a good idea.

*(***FATHER*** begins some simple stretching, as* **SON** *returns to sit near* **MOTHER.***)*

UNCLE. So when are we going to meet – sorry, what's her name again?

SON. Effi. She's really busy but, soon, I hope.

MOTHER. Just give me some notice.

SON. I'm really proud of her.

MOTHER. Well, she just, she sounds like a delight. Is she someone who – well, that's none of my business.

SON. I really love her.

MOTHER. Well, I know. You said that. And I just think it's a great, she's, just, enjoy it, okay? Cherish it.

SON. I do. When you say "delight" it makes it sound like she's a game of croquet or something.

MOTHER. Well, I certainly don't mean to say she's a game of croquet.

SON. No, it's just all these little words. I mean, how come you never ask about me, as a person?

FATHER. *(from his corner:)* Oh, we're talking about you, now?

MOTHER. So now every word I say is wrong?

SON. No, but, just, Effi is really important to me, and I want you to get to know her.

MOTHER. And I will, okay? I mean it. Just you wait and see. I promise.

UNCLE. *(brief pause)* What's she doing right now?

SON. She's studying.

UNCLE. Maybe she can join us for lunch?

SON. I don't want to bother her.

MOTHER. And this place is a mess.

SON. Maybe I'll text her and just see. *(types into his phone)*

MOTHER. I don't think it's a good day. *(to FATHER:)* Do you want us to push you back over?

FATHER. I didn't hear you.

MOTHER. I said, Do you want us to push you back over?

FATHER. Oh, then I did hear. That's what I thought you said.

MOTHER. Sandwiches from the deli isn't a very special meal.

SON. *(having read text message)* Hey, so, she really wants to take a break. I'm going to go pick her up. *(He types into his phone.)*

MOTHER. We could've planned this.

SON. Do you not want her to come?

MOTHER. I just don't like everyone disappearing.

SON. I'll be right back.

UNCLE. It'll be nice to have someone new here.

(SON gets up to put on his shoes and jacket.)

SON. Dad, do you mind if Effi comes over?

MOTHER. *(brief pause)* I don't think he heard you.

FATHER. Why do you always think I don't hear things?

MOTHER. He just wants some lunch.

FATHER. She's right.

UNCLE. We could use a little company.

SON. Yeah. Okay. I'll be right back.

MOTHER. I probably look like a mess.

SON. I just want you to meet her. All right, I'll see you later. *(as he checks pockets for his keys)* So, bye?

MOTHER. You have to tell her she's kind of taking us by surprise.

SON. I'm not going to say that.

UNCLE. See you later.

SON. Bye.

(SON exits. MOTHER glares at UNCLE.)

FATHER. Someone wheel me back.

(UNCLE wheels FATHER back to his place downstage.)

UNCLE. There we go.

MOTHER. *(brief pause)* I thought you had something to say.

FATHER. *(with frustration:)* No. I was getting tired of looking at that wall.

MOTHER. I'm not sure how I feel about strange people coming over. I wish we could've planned all this.

(MOTHER opens the gift from DAUGHTER. It's a small decorative plate. She sets it aside.)

FATHER. What is it?

MOTHER. A little plate.

(FATHER's pant-leg is a little bunched up. He tries to reach it, to push it back down, but can't.)

FATHER. My pant leg is rolled up.

MOTHER. And is that all right?

FATHER. What?

MOTHER. Did you roll it up? Is it rolled up because you wanted it like that?

FATHER. It's just my pant leg.

(UNCLE, removing the plate from its box or tissue paper:)

UNCLE. Hey, this is from Florence.

(He places it on the small stand that came with it.)

That's very thoughtful. Didn't you go there on your honeymoon?

FATHER. Venice.

MOTHER. Wasn't it Florence?

UNCLE. That's a nice gift.

FATHER. *(to* **UNCLE***:)* How would you know where we took our honeymoon?

UNCLE. No, I just remember because I always wanted to go there.

MOTHER. Did you take your second one? The antibiotic?

FATHER. Why is that the "second one"?

MOTHER. It's the second pill you take, everyday.

(Going to a drawer and taking a bottle of pills out. It's empty.)

Is this the only bottle?

FATHER. How would I know?

MOTHER. Because it's your medicine. *(looking at label)* This one's all done.

FATHER. So then someone has to go down to the drug store.

MOTHER. I wonder who that'll be.

UNCLE. I'll go down.

MOTHER. Are you sure? *(handing him the bottle)* I can go.

UNCLE. No, I could use a drive.

MOTHER. There's two refills left, so that should be fine. Do you want me to give you some money?

FATHER. Take the Club Card thing.

MOTHER. Oh, right. Take my Club Card. *(removes it from her purse and hands it to him)* There you go.

UNCLE. What does this do?

MOTHER. It gives you points.

UNCLE. What for?

FATHER. They accrue and then at the end of the year, you have a total.

MOTHER. So make sure you give them that.

UNCLE. Okay. Anything else?

MOTHER. No, I think we're fine.

UNCLE. Okay. I'll see you in a sec.

FATHER. Use that card.

UNCLE. Okay. I still don't totally get it. This isn't to pay for it, right?

FATHER. It's just for points. They accrue.

MOTHER. Do you want money?

UNCLE. No, I'll take care of it.

MOTHER. I don't think that one is very expensive.

UNCLE. All right. I'll see you later.

MOTHER. Thank you, okay?

(**UNCLE** *exits.*)

(*Brief pause.* **MOTHER** *begins working on a crossword or jigsaw puzzle.*)

FATHER. I just realized, I should've told him cranberry juice, for the morning.

MOTHER. *(not having heard:)* What?

FATHER. We need cranberry juice.

MOTHER. There's a whole thing in the fridge.

FATHER. I didn't see it.

MOTHER. It was Florence.

FATHER. I don't see what difference it makes.

MOTHER. One has canals, the other has The David. They're different places.

FATHER. Fine.

MOTHER. Remember, we saw The David. You said it looked smaller than you thought.

FATHER. Okay. You win. Fine.

MOTHER. We took a train from Rome. We didn't take any boats. I'm not trying to win, I'm saying where we took our honeymoon.

FATHER. Why are we talking about this?

MOTHER. It was a special time we spent together and I wanted to remember it with you. Correctly.

FATHER. *(without his customary edge:)* I remember you took a glass from that bar we liked. We thought they were going to come after us.

MOTHER. It was like a movie. We got in that little taxicab.

FATHER. Yeah.

MOTHER. What kind of name is Effi?

FATHER. Foreign.

MOTHER. Remember our hotel had that beautiful fountain in front of it?

FATHER. *(brief pause)* I should eat.

MOTHER. She'll be back soon. *(brief pause)* What are you thinking about?

FATHER. Why do I have to be thinking something?

MOTHER. How does it feel having the kids home?

FATHER. *(angrily, somewhat like a frustrated teenager:)* I'm fine. I'm just sitting here. I'm not like you.

MOTHER. I don't think a person can not have thoughts. But, okay.

FATHER. I didn't ask for this.

MOTHER. For what?

FATHER. What's today?

MOTHER. We went through that.

FATHER. I have a headache.

MOTHER. *(brief pause)* We didn't take any boats, so it couldn't have been Venice.

FATHER. *(frustratedly:)* Then it was the other place.

MOTHER. It's supposed to rain today? Or, when?

(He doesn't respond.)

I'll make some iced tea when she gets back.

FATHER. *(angrily:)* Fine.

MOTHER. Okay. Do we need a car battery?

(General pause. A knock at the door.)

FATHER. I bet he wants money. Or forgot his keys.

(**MOTHER** *grabs her purse and crosses to open the door.*)

MOTHER. I don't think that one is very expensive.

(Outside the door is **ANNA,** *played by actor who plays* **DAUGHTER,** *in a different costume. She is on her mobile phone and holding a bouquet of flowers in a vase.)*

*(***ANNA** *speaks into her phone, though perhaps she hasn't come into view yet.)*

ANNA. There's a stew thing I made, right in the front. Okay. *(to* **MOTHER***:)* Sorry.

(She's still standing there, in the doorway. The phone call continues.)

I know! That would be so great. No, I know! I just left them a message. I'll stay up all night, if they want the cereal bowls and the large cremation urn. So, fingers crossed. *(to* **MOTHER***:)* I'm so sorry. *(into phone, in a kind but slightly rushed effort to end the call:)* Call me if there's anything. Frank said he'd be home by five. Okay, love ya.

(She puts her phone away. Steps into the house.)

Hi. Sorry about that. That was my sister.

(She enters, so that **FATHER** *can see her.)*

(to **FATHER***:)* Hey. I heard you had some trouble. You don't remember me. It's Anna. Hi. We spoke the other week.

FATHER. Oh, right.

ANNA. These are for you. And to perk the place up a little. It's a nice orange flower, when they bloom.

(She sets the flowers down in his lap.)

FATHER. Oh. That's very thoughtful.

ANNA. Well, it's self-interest, too.

MOTHER. I'm sorry. Who are you?

ANNA. I'm Anna DeFelice. From Burlingame & West.

MOTHER. And what is that?

FATHER. She's going to sell the house for us.

MOTHER. What?

FATHER. *(to* **ANNA***:)* I told her.

ANNA. I've already had some people call.

FATHER. That's great.

MOTHER. You did not tell me.

ANNA. *(to* **MOTHER***:)* He came in the other week. We've only had a few initial conversations. *(She starts to open the curtains.)*

FATHER. Leave those closed, please.

ANNA. Let's give it a try. *(She opens a blind or curtain.)* There we go. Better already.

(Perhaps some blue sky and green trees are visible. Perhaps the effect is like a beautiful painting of the world outside, though it will take a slow and subtle change in lighting [several minutes long] to reveal this. Mainly, a different quality of light comes into the room.)

MOTHER. We weren't expecting anyone.

FATHER. So you've had some interest?

ANNA. Well, not personally, but, yes.

FATHER. What does that mean?

ANNA. *(looking through paperwork in a folder)* What does any of it mean, you know? But so, you're doing okay?

MOTHER. I think he forgets certain conversations, or remembers other ones that never happened.

ANNA. *(still looking through paperwork)* Tell me about it. Life, you know? Just forget about it. No, I'm kidding – life is one long memorable thing in a row.

FATHER. I remember conversations. I'm fine.

ANNA. Good, good. It's good to be fine. Now, personal question, you said there's a new septic system?

FATHER. Not brand new. *(to* **MOTHER***:)* You said you would miss the Winchesters.

MOTHER. What?

FATHER. You were having breakfast and you said you'd miss the Winchesters.

MOTHER. I *would* miss the Winchesters, but, we never had that conversation.

FATHER. Could we please not talk about this.

MOTHER. We never said a single word about this.

ANNA. I'm nervous, too. Please, good Lord, I understand, I get it. Change: no thank you. But, on the opposite hand, it's good, you know?

MOTHER. *(having remembered:)* I talked with David Winchester, and he said *they* were thinking about moving. And I said I'd miss them.

ANNA. I'm not surprised. The guys in my office said there's a lot of activity around. It could be a good time to sell. *(brief pause)* You didn't put in a lot of ramps around here, did you?

FATHER. No. *(referring to wheelchair)* This is only temporary.

ANNA. Good. Although, if you need a ramp I'm sure it's the most beautiful sight in the world. I have to make one quick phone call.

(She steps aside to make a call.)

MOTHER. *(brief pause)* This is our home.

FATHER. She's got it all under control.

MOTHER. I'm not worried about her. *(brief pause)* It's our home.

FATHER. Where are they with the lunch?

MOTHER. *(very brief pause)* I think I'm going to faint.

FATHER. I'm not surprised – all this traffic.

MOTHER. There's been one stable thing in my life.

FATHER. Did she leave the door open?

MOTHER. What do you care?

FATHER. *(He looks through the newspaper.)* I think this paper used to have more sections.

ANNA. *(entering, as she finishes her phone call)* Get a fifty-pound bag, if they have it. Yeah, it's "Mid-Fire Stoneware," or sometimes it says "612" on it. Okay, I love you. *(puts her* *phone away)* So... all right. *(looking around)* Now, about this. The whole, like, theme – just, all a similar color.

FATHER. What about it?

ANNA. No, it's great. But you should probably repaint.

MOTHER. I've been saying we should, for years. We even had a man come in and look.

ANNA. See? Women. Women just know.

MOTHER. But for us, though. For cheering us up, not someone else.

ANNA. As long as someone is getting cheered up, right? No, I know.

(She tidies up, a bit, moves some things around, as she speaks.)

You two need to talk. This is all delicate stuff. But, back to women. Men are fine for yelling and taking things apart, but, women just have a feeling.

FATHER. Maybe. But it's usually a feeling that, at least in my experience –

ANNA. *(interrupting:)* It's good to go with something neutral, like you have here, but just a little brighter. We can look at some paint samples. I'm interrupting – I'm sorry. I'm all over the place. I have two toddlers at home. They're with my sister. This is one of the first days I've left them both.

(She sits and starts looking through a folder.)

My littlest had a fever when I left. He said, "How come it's called a cold?" So I kind of don't care about anything else. That's not true. I'm committed to my clients. And I do pottery. I have a whole line. Here's a catalog, if you want to take a look. *(puts her catalog on an end table)* Oh, I brought some travel magazines. *(puts them on the coffee table)* It's good to have a picture of an Argentine waterfall or something on the table, while people look around. Just to put another image in their mind.

MOTHER. *(looking at the magazine cover)* That's very pretty.

(knock at the door)

FATHER. That better be lunch or medicine.

MOTHER. *(Starting to get up. To* **ANNA***:)* You don't have to explain. You're with a fellow mother and I completely understand. In fact, this is probably one of mine now.

ANNA. Oh, nice.

*(***ANNA** *moving toward door, to answer it, looking in her folder)*

(Enter **BRIAN***, played by actor who plays* **UNCLE***, in a different costume.)*

BRIAN. *(to* **MOTHER***:)* Hi. I'm Brian. Are you Anna?

ANNA. I'm Anna, right here.

BRIAN. Hi.

ANNA. *(to* **MOTHER***:)* He's just here to have a look. *(to* **BRIAN***:)* You're gonna laugh. Actually, it's not that funny. When I wrote your name down, I wrote "Brain" by accident. So when I looked at it just now, I thought, now who's this interesting person going to be? "Brain."

BRIAN. That's funny. E=MC squared?

ANNA. I know, right? So, this is the place. It is a new septic, like I thought. I was just telling these guys, one of my kids is sick, so I'm a little scattered. I mean, I'm here, and I'm excited to get going with this, but... you know, no offense.

BRIAN. No, of course.

FATHER. I take great offense.

ANNA. Oh, a wise guy. *(to* **BRIAN***:)* Did you find the place all right?

FATHER. *(with the flowers still in his lap)* Can someone take these, please?

MOTHER. *(trying to pick up the vase of flowers)* Oww. God, that hurts.

BRIAN. *(as he helpfully takes the vase from her and sets it on an end table)* Yeah, the directions were great. You okay?

ANNA. What hurts? Your wrist?

MOTHER. It's fine. *(She sits down.)*

BRIAN. *(looking around)* So, all right. Is this what color it is? I mean, no, of course it is, obviously. This is the actual color.

ANNA. Yup. This is the color. *(to* **MOTHER***:)* I tore a tendon or something in my wrist, picking up my little Phillip, and it took forever to heal. *(taking* **MOTHER***'s wrist in her hands:)* Sometimes, it felt good to press on this nerve.

MOTHER. *(partly wanting to pull her hand away)* No, that's all right, I'm fine.

ANNA. You don't sound fine.

BRIAN. *(looking around)* We'd probably need to paint. But, no, it's a nice place.

ANNA. It is. Got a lot of potential. *(still gently massaging* **MOTHER***'s wrist)* Just breathe. It seems like it might be a nerve thing. *(to* **BRIAN***:)* Yeah, some paint would perk things up. And of course you'll want to do an inspection. But I think it's generally in good shape.

FATHER. It's in very good shape.

ANNA. *(to* **MOTHER***:)* How's it feel?

MOTHER. That's very nice, actually.

BRIAN. *(looking at the vase of flowers)* Those are pretty.

> *(He turns the vase, so that the color and beauty of the flowers is even more prominently visible to the audience. Or, a production can use battery-powered "magic" plastic flowers that bloom over the course of ten or fifteen minutes.)*

We can do this another time.

MOTHER. That's all right. We were just sitting here.

BRIAN. Well, okay – if you were just sitting here. *(Sits down on couch. Looking at coffee table magazines.)* Oh, wow, is that Iguazu?

ANNA. You know what, I think you're right. I never know, is that in Argentina or Brazil? Because I believe the Iguazu River forms the border.

BRIAN. Don't ask me – my name is just Brian. Do you travel?

ANNA. Just here and there.

FATHER. That describes everywhere. Going "here and there" is the definition of travel.

BRIAN. So it is.

(FATHER *picks up his newspaper.*)

(*to* ANNA:) I think that's a nice way to describe it. *(looking at catalog)* This is beautiful pottery. *(leafs through it)* Hey, that's you!

ANNA. I'll give you one of those, if you want to look.

BRIAN. I do. Oh, and did you bring stuff about the house on Bedford Road?

ANNA. Yup, that's out in my car. We can take a look at that one, too.

(ANNA *is still massaging* MOTHER*'s wrist.*)

MOTHER. Oh that feels so much better. Thank you. You're like an angel.

ANNA. No, sure. I hate when stuff hurts. *(to* BRIAN:) I actually brought the travel magazines over. Full disclosure.

BRIAN. No, I figured someone left it here. When I was a little kid, I worried I couldn't make shovels work. I just was too light, but I didn't understand that, and it made me cry. Full disclosure.

ANNA. I'm so glad you told me that.

BRIAN. I didn't want you to hear it out on the street.

(*They share a little smile over the joke.*)

MOTHER. It almost makes me see nice different colors, when you press on that.

ANNA. I'm glad.

FATHER. Remember I said it was probably a nerve?

MOTHER. *(a little dismissively:)* Did you?

BRIAN. You should meet my wife.

MOTHER. Well, I would love to meet her.

BRIAN. You made me think of her, when you said that about a nice color in your mind.

MOTHER. Does she have that happen, too? Oh, that feels so good.

ANNA. *(to* **BRIAN***:)* And there's a nice yard, you saw that, right?

MOTHER. *(to* **BRIAN***:)* What does she do, your wife?

(cordless "home phone" rings)

Sorry, one sec – hold that thought.

*(***MOTHER*** *goes off-stage to answer phone.)*

BRIAN. *(to* **FATHER***:)* Can I ask why you're selling?

FATHER. No.

BRIAN. Can I ask a follow-up question?

*(***FATHER*** *returns to his newspaper.)*

BRIAN. *(with understanding:)* You're busy.

ANNA. So, what was I saying? There's the very nice yard, and, it's a good neighborhood.

*(***MOTHER*** *partly enters room.)*

MOTHER. *(to* **FATHER***:)* What kind of car does Susie drive? *(into phone:)* It's blue. Yes. I think it's one of those little blue Fords. Can I speak to her? Okay. I'll be right there. Thank you. *(puts the phone down)*

ANNA. Is everything okay?

MOTHER. Well, I don't know. I hope so.

FATHER. Who was that?

MOTHER. I think she's had an accident. My daughter.

ANNA. Oh no.

BRIAN. Is she okay?

MOTHER. They said she was all right, but, I couldn't talk to her.

ANNA. I'll go with you.

MOTHER. No, that's all right. *(preparing to leave)* But – oh, God – we're waiting for medicine for him.

ANNA. Of course. That's no problem. I'll stay here and make sure he's all right. *(hands her a business card)* Just call if you need anything. I'll stay right here.

MOTHER. Okay. God. Thank you.

BRIAN. I should get out of your way.

ANNA. No, could you stay? Just for a little bit.

BRIAN. Sure.

ANNA. *(to* **MOTHER***:)* I know you're scared. I hope she's okay. They said she was, right?

MOTHER. Yes.

ANNA. But I know you won't feel all right until you see her.

(The next is said in a much more simple and quiet and connected way than we have heard from **MOTHER** *before. Perhaps because of the simple touch and attention given to her by* **ANNA.***)*

MOTHER. I've driven by car crashes and I'm imagining it all and all the loud noises and she just, she shouldn't be there. Oh. She glued some seashells and a little statue on the dashboard. And I'm imagining everything all over the place and her car all smashed up. All the little things we do look so sweet and innocent when something bad happens. All the fixing up.

ANNA. Yeah. That's a nice thought.

BRIAN. She'll be really glad to see you.

MOTHER. You know, my wrist doesn't hurt for the first time in ages. I feel like a different person. I'm not being a terrible mother, sitting here. They said it would be a little while before I could see her. *(very brief pause)* Oh, God, I hope she's all right.

ANNA. Well, get down there and find out for sure.

MOTHER. I will. Are you sure you'll be alright here?

ANNA. No, we'll be fine.

BRIAN. *(as* **MOTHER** *is exiting)* Here, take this. *(small laugh)* I don't know why I'm giving you gum. But, maybe you'll want some gum.

MOTHER. *(surprisingly moved, as she's checking for her keys:)* Maybe I will. Thank you. Maybe I'll have it on the drive over there. *(She looks at it.)* "Antarctic Mint." It sounds delicious. *(She looks at the wrapper.)* Polar bears. Excuse me. Thank you. *(begins leaving)*

ANNA. Okay. Let us know, okay? *(to* **FATHER**:*)* Do you want to say anything?

FATHER. Wouldn't I have said it?

*(**MOTHER** exits. **BRIAN** stands in the doorway to make sure she gets to her car.)*

BRIAN. *(to* **ANNA**:*)* So, do you know the daughter?

ANNA. I really just know him. And not very well.

FATHER. "Him?"

ANNA. Sorry. Hi. How're you doing?

FATHER. What do you want me to say?

ANNA. Just, how you're doing.

BRIAN. Cars are the most normal thing in the world, but when our son got his license, it suddenly seemed like he was going around in this experimental contraption.

ANNA. I can't even imagine. *(to* **FATHER**:*)* Do you want a water?

(Gets a bottle of Poland Spring water out of her bag and puts it down near **FATHER***, and puts some bottles on the coffee table.)*

My husband got me these. It's Polish mineral water. It's good.

*(**BRIAN** opens the door upstage, that we have never seen open. Some more light and air enter the stage, as he disappears into this back room, perhaps flicking a light on and off and on, back there. Knock at the door. **TOM**, played by actor who plays **SON**, enters. He's wearing landscaper/painter type clothes. He has a box of pastries. **BRIAN** has gone into another part of the house.)*

TOM. It's me. Hi. This was open.

ANNA. *(as she's looking through her folder)* Hi, Tom. Thanks for coming.

TOM. No, sure. I brought some… I'll put these here. *(places the pastries down)*

ANNA. Wow, great.

FATHER. Who's this?

TOM. She just said my name. Hi.

ANNA. Tom does some work for me, painting and landscaping. I wanted him to have a look in here and at the yard and maybe give you some thoughts.

TOM. Totally.

ANNA. But, their daughter's had a car accident, so maybe this isn't the best time.

TOM. Oh, no. Is she all right?

ANNA. *(very brief pause)* We think so. We're waiting to hear. Her mom just left to go find out.

TOM. *(to* **FATHER***:)* Man. I'm sorry.

FATHER. Did you close the door?

TOM. I hope she's all right.

> *(**FATHER**'s blanket has dropped off his knees, earlier.)*

FATHER. Can someone get the blanket.

TOM. Sure.

> *(He hands it to him. To* **FATHER***, whispered, kind of coldly, and eerily:)*

Remember me?

ANNA. What?

TOM. *(to* **FATHER***:)* I hope your daughter's all right. *(to* **ANNA***:)* I remember being over at your house one time when the kids had ear infections.

ANNA. *(sympathetic laugh)* Oh, man, that was a scene. The poor little guys. They were just screaming and screaming. And then they started making animal noises, and then Frank, and then we all started.

TOM. *(cow sound:)* Moooo.

BRIAN. *(from somewhere else in the house:)* Mooooo!

ANNA. *(a quick small laugh)* But, God, I remember that. It's so hard. *(sort of to* **FATHER***:)* You hold a little person, you stroke their hair or make cocoa or something, and you think it's all better but there's still this pain in their head you can't make go away. *(Very brief pause. A difficult memory she tries to shake off:)* Oh.

*(***BRIAN*** re-enters.)*

BRIAN. *(to* **TOM***:)* Hi.

TOM. Hey.

FATHER. Today's my anniversary.

ANNA. Nice. Of what?

FATHER. My wedding anniversary.

TOM. Congrats.

BRIAN. Congratulations. *(drifts off again into another room)*

FATHER. Our dog ran away.

TOM. *(as he's looking around or making a note in his notepad)* Oh, okay – we're getting the whole life story.

ANNA. Have you called the dog catcher?

FATHER. *(frustratedly:)* No, we haven't called the dog catcher.

ANNA. Oh. Shouldn't you?

FATHER. You're worse than my wife.

TOM. Hey, don't talk about people like that.

FATHER. Are you threatening me?

TOM. I guess so, if you want to just blast right up to that next level.

ANNA. It's all right, Tom. He's had a big day.

FATHER. I have not had a big day. You're going to threaten a person in a wheelchair?

TOM. Well, no, when you say it like that.

FATHER. This is my house and I'll say who is worse than who.

TOM. I might threaten an asshole who's a bully in a wheelchair, though.

(The following exchange happens quickly.)

FATHER. Don't you use language like that in here.

TOM. *(moving toward FATHER, to sit down next to him)* I'll say any word I know.

ANNA. Tom. Come on, it's okay.

FATHER. You have no respect.

TOM. Yeah, that's right, I don't.

FATHER. *(to ANNA:)* This is who you bring in here?

ANNA. I've known Tom a long time.

TOM. I've taken a lot of drugs. In my life, and, earlier today. I keep little liquor bottles in my glove compartment.

FATHER. So?

TOM. I'm just telling you where I'm at, as a person.

FATHER. This is my house. You're in my house.

TOM. This is MY house. *(brief pause)* I'm kidding. You're right, it's your house.

FATHER. You have no right.

TOM. *(to ANNA:)* I don't really take drugs. I mean, sure, pot and cocaine and alcohol and stuff like that.

ANNA. Oh, I don't care about that. I appreciate you being… Just, the poor man's been through a lot, whether he knows it or not.

TOM. You're right.

FATHER. Don't talk about me like I'm not here.

ANNA. Okay.

(Brief pause. BRIAN re-appears from another room.)

BRIAN. Is there a basement?

ANNA. *(to FATHER:)* Is there a basement?

FATHER. It's a house, isn't it?

BRIAN. I'll just take a look.

(opens the closet door, immediately closes it)

That's a closet.

ANNA. There's a lot of closet space.

(BRIAN drifts off, again, to inspect another room.)

TOM. *(to FATHER:)* Hey, so, we got off on the wrong foot.

FATHER. That's it?

TOM. Pretend I just walked out and then walked back in. Hi. I'm just here to look around and tell Anna or you or any potential buyer what I, as a painter and landscaper, think.

FATHER. Fine.

ANNA. *(to FATHER:)* You're probably tired.

FATHER. So now you're a doctor?

ANNA. Nope, I'm not a doctor. *(to BRIAN, who has re-appeared:)* Anyway. So?

BRIAN. No, it's nice.

TOM. *(to ANNA:)* I'm sorry if I flew off the handle.

ANNA. It's okay.

TOM. No, I'm an idiot.

FATHER. Well, that's the first intelligent –

(TOM interrupts him by making a very loud beeping sound, sort of like the 'flatline' sound from an EKG monitor:)

TOM. Beeeeeeeeeeppppppppp. *(amused with himself:)* I don't know why I did that. It was probably weird – it just came to me, to make a beeping sound.

BRIAN	**ANNA**
(amused:) Beeeeepppp.	*(amused:)* Dooot.

BRIAN. It's a good way to cut someone off.

ANNA. It is. I didn't know what was going on.

BRIAN. So, yeah. Can I look around a little more?

FATHER. No.

ANNA. He's kidding. Please.

(She gestures for him to go look. BRIAN goes over to the stairs. Hesitates, maybe points up, as if to say, "Can I go up here?", then starts up stairs. Third stair squeaks, he stops for a moment, makes it squeak one more time.)

TOM. *(inspecting the back wall)* So, this is wallpaper.

ANNA. I know. Would you have to go all the way down to the sheetrock?

TOM. These ones are actually plaster.

ANNA. Oh, nice.

TOM. Do you want me to pull up a little section?

ANNA. *(to FATHER:)* Can he pull up a little wallpaper?

FATHER. I feel strange.

TOM. That wasn't the question.

ANNA. C'mon – be nice. *(to FATHER:)* Just to have a look? *(to TOM:)* I'm sure it's fine. *(occupied with reading from her folder, to FATHER:)* So how long have you guys… How long have you been living here?

(TOM peels down a little wallpaper, then a little more, revealing a gorgeous but faded wallpaper underneath. ANNA quietly registers this, in a happy we-shouldn't-be-doing-this way.)

TOM. Hey, look at that.

ANNA. Oh, I like that. They should just have that. *(whispers:)* Can you do one more? *(He quietly peels back another strip.)* That's really pretty.

(BRIAN entering:)

BRIAN. Yeah, that's nice. You really have to be committed to put up wallpaper. It's like gluing this ideal of yourself all over the house.

FATHER. *(seeing the wallpaper)* That was here originally. Or, no. Maybe my wife picked it out.

ANNA. She did a nice job. *(to BRIAN:)* What do you think of the rest of the place?

BRIAN. It's good.

ANNA. The stairs squeak. Which you noticed.

BRIAN. We have a teenage boy, so it's good to have squeaky stairs. But, yeah, it's nice. *(to TOM:)* Although, let me ask you, can you remove tear stains? I'm kidding. *(to FATHER:)* I'm kidding. It's nice.

ANNA. I have some other properties. But this was the best of the bunch, in your range. Also, the Bedford Road place. We'll take a look at that.

(She and TOM *sit down. She takes a bite of a pastry.)*

These are good.

TOM. They're from that place.

ANNA. They're good. *(to* BRIAN:*)* But, yeah, you could do a lot here.

BRIAN. It's funny. A house is kind of a house. I mean, it's exactly a house.

(perhaps resting his hand on FATHER*'s wheelchair)*

I don't know how it happened, but, my wife and I, Melissa, we suddenly became, kind of behind our own backs, pretty spiritual people.

(Perhaps, as he gestures in a small way with his hand, he momentarily blocks the audience's view of FATHER*'s face.)*

Not in a church way, at all, but, just, I don't know how to say it, just, busy with stuff that isn't material.

ANNA. Like what?

BRIAN. *(moving toward them to sit down, gesturing to pastry:)* Can I grab –

ANNA. Um – Tom brought these.

TOM. Help yourself.

*(*BRIAN *grabs a pastry.)*

BRIAN. I haven't eaten all day. *(He takes a bite.)* So she's gotten into chanting, all the different chants that different people have. I mean, everyone, Buddhist monks and basketball fans, how kids tease each other on a playground, and crazy things like the mantras they sing during Tibetan Sky Burials. There was just a documentary on –

TOM. *(interrupting:)* I saw that. *(to* ANNA:*)* Have you heard of these things? I guess Tibet is mostly rock, so they do this thing where they leave the body out –

BRIAN. *(interrupting:)* Sometimes they mash it to a pulp or hack it all apart into arms and legs and a torso.

TOM. Right, yeah. It's awesome. And they just leave it out for the vultures and birds and animals. They just let it decompose and get eaten.

FATHER. I don't like this.

TOM. Well, if you're not dead, you don't have to worry about it.

BRIAN. Or Tibetan. Anyway, it's supposed to help you move from this world to the next, getting rid of your corporeal body. And spreading it out through the wild.

ANNA. That's intense.

TOM. That's the funny thing.

ANNA. Oh, good – there's a funny thing.

(She exits into what must be the kitchen to get some paper towels for everyone. She returns fairly quickly.)

TOM. *(speaking up, so ANNA can hear him)* Well, no, but, they showed people getting the body ready, and they were just laughing and talking, like they were carving a pumpkin or painting a fence or something. It's done by either monks or just a family who's in that business.

BRIAN. They have a different relation to the whole thing. You come, you go, you were never really here. And so she's – she being Melissa – she's comparing all these chants to see if there's one unifying principle. They actually all look similar, when you see the soundwaves on a computer. Anyway, so there's that. And I've been designing furniture. I haven't built any of it, yet, and that's kind of part of it. It's fun to just draw something and then wonder if it would be nice to theoretically sit in. And we still have the restaurant. *(to TOM:)* We own a restaurant.

TOM. Yum. I was just at a restaurant this morning.

(Knock at the door. MELISSA, played by the actor who plays MOTHER, appears at the door, in a different costume, chewing gum. ANNA gets up to greet her.)

MELISSA. Hello? I don't know if I'm at the right –

BRIAN. Hey, sweetheart. This is Melissa. I was just talking about you.

MELISSA. Hi, honey. Are you Anna?

ANNA. I am. Hi, Melissa.

TOM. *(passing her at the door)* Hi. Tom. I have to run out to my truck. *(exits)*

BRIAN. *(eating a pastry)* Sit down. Have one of these.

MELISSA. Oh, yummy. Thank you.

(She doesn't eat one. To **BRIAN***:)*

So, have you looked around?

BRIAN. *(in a calming and respectful tone:)* Their daughter had a car accident. So it's a little stressful around here. They think she's all right.

MELISSA. Oh, no – I'm sorry. We can do all this another time.

ANNA. I think it's okay. Her mother just left for the hospital. I'm staying, in case there's anything I can do. And we're waiting for some medicine for, um… *(She motions toward* **FATHER***.)*

MELISSA. Oh. *(to* **FATHER***, from behind his back:)* I hope everything's all right.

FATHER. Who just walked in? Is that her?

ANNA. Um, yup. It's Melissa. Melissa is here with Brian.

FATHER. All these names.

ANNA. You okay?

FATHER. How many of you are there?

MELISSA. It's like a party. No, don't worry. We won't touch anything.

BRIAN. Anyway, I was telling Anna and Tom about how we're, yeah, I don't know – a roof over our head, and we're probably fine.

ANNA. Hang on, let me check the specs, here. *(She looks in her folder.)* Yeah, just as I thought – this place has a roof.

BRIAN. I know! I saw it when I drove up.

MELISSA. And I like that it has walls. No, seriously, this could be cute. *(somewhat quieter voice:)* But we should look at that other place.

ANNA. Yup. Of course. Brian said. We can look at that later. *(checking folder)* Today's Tuesday, right? *(or whatever day it presently is)*

BRIAN. All day.

MELISSA. That's such a nice sound. "Tuesday." *(or whatever day it presently is)*

(TOM enters. Maybe for a moment, we don't know whether he is playing a new character or is the SON returning. He stands at the door. Brief pause.)

TOM. What was I doing? *(brief pause)* Tape measure. *(He exits.)*

FATHER. I can't tell if I'm dizzy.

ANNA. I know the feeling.

FATHER. No, you do not know the feeling. *(very brief pause)* Where is everyone?

ANNA. There's a whole room full of people right here.

FATHER. Do you hear me saying this?

MELISSA. Of course. Are you all right?

FATHER. *(simply, and with a simple fear, perhaps like a child:)* Why are you asking me if I'm all right?

MELISSA. Well, I'm worried. But, you're doing okay? *(Brief pause. To FATHER:)* I want you to smile, all right? Can you smile?

BRIAN. What?

MELISSA. It's one of the things you ask. *(to FATHER:)* I'm just going to do this, okay? *(TOM enters. She checks his pulse.)* His heart is going a mile a minute. Do you have any kind of history with heart trouble?

FATHER. No.

MELISSA. Can you hear me?

FATHER. No.

MELISSA. Does anything feel strange? Like, in your neck or shoulders, or maybe your jaw?

FATHER. My jaw. And my neck.

ANNA. I'm calling an ambulance, right now.

(She steps away and calls.)

MELISSA. I think that makes sense. Do you have aspirin? Can someone find an aspirin?

TOM. I'll look. *(He exits, up the stairs.)*

BRIAN. Is it a heart attack?

MELISSA. I'm not sure. *(to FATHER:)* How you doing? *(Brief pause. Reassuringly:)* It's going to be okay. This is a nice sunny room, huh?

ANNA. They're coming right away.

MELISSA. *(to ANNA:)* You said you were waiting for something for him. What medication is he on?

(ANNA is still on hold with the emergency phone call, perhaps waiting for a last piece of administrative information.)

ANNA. I don't know. I literally just walked in the door, ten minutes ago.

BRIAN. *(to FATHER:)* You okay? *(to ANNA:)* She did CPR training, because of the restaurant.

MELISSA. Well, but it was three years ago.

ANNA. The hospital is really close. They're just down the street.

MELISSA. Yeah, don't worry. Everything's going to be okay.

ANNA. Shopping and public transportation are also very close.

(They all stifle a little laughter.)

I'm sorry.

MELISSA. *(to FATHER:)* Aren't we awful. *(Brief pause. Mainly to FATHER:)* But it's nice to be right near everything, isn't it? In case you need to run out for milk or something.

(**ANNA** *quietly ends phone call with 911. "Okay. Thank you."*)

BRIAN. I like the look of that deli.

ANNA. The Blue Rooster. That place is great.

TOM. *(enters, with aspirin)* Here.

MELISSA. I want you to take this, okay? *(to others:)* I think it's good, just as a precaution.

(**FATHER** *nods, swallows aspirin.*)

FATHER. This was our house.

MELISSA. It still is. It's very nice. I'm sure you're just sitting here feeling all the different feelings you felt here. It's always hard to say goodbye to a house. *(brief pause)* They'll be here soon. Just breathe.

FATHER. I am breathing.

MELISSA. I'm sorry, you're right – I'm just saying the silly things people say.

BRIAN. *(to MELISSA:)* You're being great.

ANNA. No, I know, I'm so glad you're here. *(sound of ambulance approaching)*

BRIAN. Should we get him out front?

MELISSA. That's a good idea. Can you help?

TOM. Of course.

MELISSA. Maybe it's better if we don't move him.

BRIAN. *(to FATHER:)* They're going to be here any second.

FATHER. Move me.

TOM. You want to go outside?

(**FATHER** *nods.*)

Why don't we just bring him out there, so it's quicker.

MELISSA. I guess so. If he wants you to.

(**TOM** *and* **BRIAN** *start to wheel him out the door. Sound of ambulance pulling up outside.*)

FATHER. My glasses.

MELISSA. Here, take his glasses. Just put them in that back pocket.

(**TOM** *tucks the glasses in a pocket on the back of the wheelchair.*)

TOM. *(to* **FATHER***:)* Your glasses are right back here, okay? All right, let's get you outside.

ANNA. I'll tell your wife where you are. (**BRIAN** *and* **TOM** *wheel* **FATHER** *out the door.*)

MELISSA. *(a pause)* Oh, and there was a blanket, too. *(She picks it up off the floor.)* You know what, it would probably just get lost. *(She folds it up and lays it on the couch.)*

ANNA. *(pause)* Wow. This is not how these things usually go. Usually I set out cheese and crackers and maybe somebody has an allergy attack because of pets or something. I'm sure this isn't how anyone wants to see their potential home. I'm sorry.

MELISSA. It's a house with people in it – there's nothing to apologize about.

(sound of ambulance siren, pulling away)

Do you have a number for his wife?

ANNA. Oh, and I just remembered, the poor daughter. *(checking her phone)* I think I just have the number for here.

MELISSA. Do they have other kids?

ANNA. I don't know.

(**TOM** *enters, with* **BRIAN.***)*

TOM. I always think it's a good sign, when they turn the siren on, on the way back.

BRIAN. "Always"? Do you do a lot of loading people into ambulances?

TOM. I guess it depends on what you'd call "a lot."

ANNA. He looked so scared.

MELISSA. Didn't he. God. The poor man. What did he want his glasses for, you know? I hope he's all right.

ANNA. How old are your kids? Brian said you had children. Oh – I wrote his name down "Brain," by accident.

MELISSA. *(little laugh)* I actually call him "Brain" sometimes.

BRIAN. True story. I mean, I don't know if that really has the elements of a "story," *per se.* But, yeah, Charlotte is 12 and our son Mark is 17.

MELISSA. They think we're both losers, but, they're sweet kids.

ANNA. I'd be so hurt if my kids didn't like me.

BRIAN. No, they like us, they just get moody. They just get a little yell-y.

MELISSA. *(looking at removed wallpaper)* Are they painting?

ANNA. We were just taking a look at the walls.

TOM. I can put that back up with some tape.

ANNA. Yeah, maybe later. That's probably the least of their worries right now.

MELISSA. That's such a pretty pattern.

BRIAN. We were just saying that. *(very brief pause)* So, what do you think? I called Charles.

MELISSA. Oh, good. *(looking around)* I like it. I don't know. I like it.

ANNA. I might just pick up a little bit, so it's nice and neat when they get back.

(Everyone sort of joins in on the straightening up. Perhaps MELISSA *puts away the phone that* MOTHER *left out. Perhaps* ANNA *folds up wrapping paper from the gift* DAUGHTER *gave* MOTHER.*)*

BRIAN. So you said this was a slightly different situation. How ready are they to sell, do you think?

ANNA. They're close. But, yeah. I thought things were a little in flux, before, and now, you know, now this.

BRIAN. Yeah, of course.

MELISSA. What do you mean, in flux?

ANNA. I don't know. I guess he hadn't really talked with her about moving and it just seemed like something was brewing.

BRIAN. Do you mean like a divorce?

ANNA. I really don't know, but, maybe.

MELISSA. Would that – sorry, kind of a crude question, but – would it complicate the sale process?

ANNA. It might, to be honest. I'm not sure.

MELISSA. My brother's a lawyer. We can ask him.

TOM. *(putting something away into a drawer of an end table)* Hey, check it out – photo album.

BRIAN. Oh, let's look.

MELISSA. That's none of our business, Brain.

BRIAN. Just because maybe there's pictures of the house. Renovations and stuff.

ANNA. Yeah, let's see.

(They all gather around **TOM** *on the couch, in sort of a tableau. He opens the album.)*

TOM. Hey, this is old Main Street. Look at the cars. *(flips one page ahead, and then through the rest)* There's only two pictures.

BRIAN. I was ready for a whole trip back in time.

MELISSA. Look at that dog. Cute. The little ribbon.

BRIAN. Don't let Charlotte see that. *(to* **ANNA***:)* Our daughter wants a dog.

MELISSA. *(a little smile)* The other day, he says to her, "When you're twenty-five."

BRIAN. I said thirty-five. It's a lot of responsibility.

ANNA. I need to get some of those photo albums.

*(***CHARLES***, played by actor who plays* **FATHER***, has quietly appeared at the door and has been staring at them for a little while. He is in shorts and a sweaty t-shirt, having just done a workout or some jogging.)*

CHARLES. Anybody home?

MELISSA. Hey, Charlie. This is my brother.

BRIAN. Charles.

ANNA. Hi, I'm Anna. I'm the realtor.

CHARLES. Hi, how are you.

MELISSA. Thanks for getting all dressed up.

CHARLES. As your lawyer, I'm going to recommend that you don't make fun of my clothes. *(to* **TOM***:)* Hey, I know this guy.

TOM. Hey, man.

BRIAN. How do you guys know each other?

CHARLES. He painted my office, or, he was going to paint it.

TOM. Yeah, did that all work out?

CHARLES. It's fine. Sorry, what's your name?

TOM. Tom.

CHARLES. Tom, I'm Charles Weisscamp. *(sits down, makes himself at home)* So, what do we think?

MELISSA. I don't know. It's sweet.

CHARLES. *(looking at the gift plate)* I like this plate.

MELISSA. Yeah, it's very pretty.

CHARLES. *(noticing the partially stripped wallpaper)* What's happening here?

ANNA. We did that.

TOM. The walls are in pretty good shape.

CHARLES. *(notices wrapping paper)* What's this? Was it someone's birthday?

TOM. It's their anniversary. The guy said.

BRIAN. So, speaking of that, "ker-clunk," not a great segue, but, does a divorce usually mess up home sales?

CHARLES. Usually. Not necessarily, though. Nothing necessarily messes up anything.

ANNA. I really shouldn't have said that. I don't know for sure.

CHARLES. So where are they? *(quieter voice:)* Are they here?

MELISSA. Oh, the poor things. The man is at the hospital. He might've had a stroke or a heart thing. And their daughter got into a car accident and the mother's – I wonder if – yeah, I guess maybe they're all over at the hospital.

CHARLES. Wow. That's a lot.

ANNA. I know.

CHARLES. At least they're together.

TOM. It's weird, being here. You know? *(very brief pause)* We are the people who are here.

ANNA. Yeah? I think you need to stop sneaking out to your truck.

TOM. What do you mean?

ANNA. Maybe you shouldn't drink and smoke pot during work.

TOM. No, yeah, that makes sense.

MELISSA. *(to BRIAN:)* Can you picture us here?

BRIAN. Hang on.

(He closes his eyes, and imagines them all sitting there.)

Yeah. I can. *(to TOM:)* I have sort of a gift.

CHARLES. How's the rest of the place?

BRIAN. It's nice.

MELISSA. It's got potential.

CHARLES. *(crossing to look out the window)* Every house has potential, but, potential for what?

ANNA. *(checking specs)* I think it's a new washer and drier.

BRIAN. *(to MELISSA:)* You should look around.

MELISSA. I could kind of see us here.

(She opens the closet door.)

Oops.

(Closes it, leaving it partly open. A nice dash of color is visible, perhaps a yellow raincoat is hanging on the inside of the closet door. Perhaps there is also a map drawn by a child, hanging there.)

Did you look upstairs? *(brief pause)* What was that? Did you hear that? Is someone else here?

(A somewhat eerie pause. Everyone stays very still and listens.)

BRIAN. Old house. It's probably just settling.

TOM. Houses don't actually settle. It's more the earth rising up around them.

CHARLES. *(as if he just felt a chill, recognizing the gravity of the thought:)* Brrrr… Dark thoughts from a home improvement specialist.

TOM. No, it's true. I saw a thing about it.

CHARLES. I believe you. I'm just not sure that houses being swallowed up by the earth is what my sister wants to be thinking about when she's looking at a new place.

BRIAN. *(genially disagreeing:)* Well, I don't know about that.

MELISSA. Yeah, I think it's something to consider.

CHARLES. Okay. But, anyway, I think this'd be nice. You guys could definitely be – it's sappy, I won't say it.

BRIAN. It's got a nice yard, out back. I was looking from upstairs.

TOM. *(referring to whatever **CHARLES** was going to say:)* What?

MELISSA. Charlie thinks we're a great family. He was probably going to say we'd be happy anywhere.

CHARLES. *(to **TOM**:)* No, I was going to say, "They're all awful people and they'll be miserable wherever they go."

ANNA. Well, then, it sounds like you'd be fine here, either way.

MELISSA. Maybe. *(to **CHARLES**, laughing:)* You don't think that.

CHARLES. How big is the lot? *(looking out the window)* Hey, there's a little dog out there.

(**MELISSA** *moves to the window.* **BRIAN** *leans in the front doorway, looking out, his back to the audience.*)

Hey, little fella.

ANNA. *(checking her folder)* It's half an acre.

MELISSA. That's so funny – he's just sitting there. Hey, sweetie.

(Perhaps there's a very subtle change in the lighting, and even perhaps a very subtle music cue, to suggest that the play is ending at this particular moment. Again, if this is done, it should be done almost subliminally, so that we feel the play is going to end without us seeing the dog.)

BRIAN. Hey, buddy.

(A dog enters, wagging its tail and greeting everyone.)

TOM. Hey, who's this?

ANNA. I'm sort of allergic. He's a cutie, though.

TOM. I think it's a she.

*(**MELISSA** kneels down to pat him.)*

MELISSA. Hello, sweetie. Are you lost? What a pretty dog. Aren't you. Aren't you.

(blackout)

End

ALTERNATE ENDING

This version of the end of the play does not use a real dog. It begins with MELISSA's line toward the bottom of page 68.

MELISSA. Maybe. *(to CHARLES, laughing:)* You don't think that.

CHARLES. How big is the lot? *(looking out the window)* Hey, there's a little dog out there.

(Everyone's attention is drawn to the window or door.)

Hey, little fella.

MELISSA. That's so funny – he's just sitting there. Hey, sweetie.

BRIAN. Hey, buddy.

ANNA. He's a cutie.

(They've all arranged themselves so that they're looking out the windows and door. BRIAN is leaning in the doorway. ANNA and TOM are near the couch, but turned away from the audience, looking out the window or door. It would be a perfectly welcoming scene, if a person were walking toward the house, but the audience will see it from the back, with all of the actors mainly facing away from them, looking off toward the back and stage-right or stage-left.)

TOM. I think it's a she.

MELISSA. Hello, sweetie. Are you lost? What a pretty dog. Aren't you. Aren't you.

(blackout)

End

71

CPSIA information can be obtained at www.ICGtesting.com
Printed in the USA
LVOW04s1140250815

451454LV00023B/318/P